ISLAND OF ADVENTURES

Fun things to do all around

★ **IRELAND** ★

Aunty Ava

Jack

Sea Stack Climbing & Hillwalking

Northern Lights

Whale & Dolphin Watching

Stand-Up Paddle Boarding

Donegal

Horse Trekking

Belfast

Shipwreck Diving

Boating

Sandcastle Championship

Westport

Newgrange

ATLANTIC OCEAN

St. Patrick's Day

Galway

Athlone

Hot Air Balloon

Phoenix Park Deer

Dublin

River Shannon

IRISH SEA

Fleadh Ceoil

Haunted Castle

Surfing & Bodyboarding

Limerick

Mountain Biking

Wexford

Seal Spotting

Dingle

Fota Wildlife

Puck Fair

Cork

Bird Watching Skelligs

Starlight Kayak

ISLAND OF ADVENTURES
This map shows just some of the locations where you can have an exciting adventure. Many of these activities can be enjoyed all over Ireland.

ISLAND OF ADVENTURES

Fun things to do all around IRELAND

Jennifer Farley

THE O'BRIEN PRESS
DUBLIN

Deer Spotting In Dublin

The Phoenix Park in Dublin is the biggest walled city park in Europe. There are tons of fun things to do there, including visiting Dublin Zoo and the President of Ireland's house.

A very special adventure you can have in the park is to view the wild fallow deer. There has been a herd of deer living in the Phoenix Park since the 17th century. They were once hunted for food and enjoyment, but today the deer are protected and they roam freely throughout the park. Most of the time you can see them in the area known as the Fifteen Acres.

Áras an Uachtaráin   **Home of the President**

Male deer, called bucks, fight fiercely using their antlers.

A baby deer is a fawn.

4

While the deer are used to seeing and being near to people, it's important to remember that they are still wild animals, so they can be unpredictable. Also very important, don't feed them! Deer have plenty of their own natural food and don't need anything from us.

Has there been an escape at Dublin Zoo?

A female deer is a doe.

Park Ranger & Deer Keeper.

Keep dogs on a lead around the deer.

The deer in the Phoenix Park are fallow deer.

A humpback whale's tail can be 3.5m wide.

Harbour Porpoise

Bottlenose Dolphins eat fish, crabs and squid.

Mackerel is a favourite food of dolphins in Irish waters.

Basking Shark

Diver

Fin Whale

Humpback Whale

Watch Whales & Dolphins

Lucky for us, and for our visitors to Ireland, our waters are teeming with amazing wildlife. Whales, sharks and dolphins swim around our coastline.

   You can go whale and dolphin watching from the land or from a boat. Obviously, you can get much closer to them from a boat, but there are many areas along the coast where you can see marine life swimming by. Get up high on a coastal hill or a cliff and you may see a gentle giant out at sea. If you're on a boat, the guide will tell you what to look out for, such as feeding seabirds, flocking around feeding whales.

   And it's not only in summer that we get to see these magnificent marine creatures. There are many species passing through our waters all year round including the giant Fin Whale – the second biggest animal on the planet after the Blue Whale. Grab your binoculars and get to the coast!

Mountain Biking – Let's Go Off-Road!

With our gorgeous hills, forests and mountains, Ireland is a perfect playground for cyclists who want to get off the main road and get dirty. There are mountain bike trails all over the country – some are hard and some are easy. If the thought of travelling downhill through a forest at speed leaves you with a big smile on your face, then mountain biking is the adventure for you.

Woodpecker

Red Squirrel

If you're a beginner, you can learn how to use your brakes – no flying over the handlebars, learn how to go uphill and stay in your seat, learn how to go downhill staying focused and relaxed and learn how to stay in control of your bike with all kinds of obstacles coming your way!

Or, if mountains and mud aren't your thing, but you love to cycle, you can try some of the beautiful greenways around the country.

Got your helmet? Got your bike? Let's hit the trail!

Stoat

Pine Marten

Mountain bikers carry
spare tubes, tools, a
pump and a first aid kit
in their backpacks.

Peacock Butterfly

Leisler's Bat are the biggest bats in Ireland (but they're actually really small).

Long-eared owl

Badger

Hedgehog

A baby bat is called a pup.

Visit A Haunted House

Ireland is a land of myths and legends. Some happy, some sad and some scary. Throughout the land there are many haunted houses and castles. Local people tell stories of ghosts, banshees, vampires and of hearing piercing screams at night!

One such spooky place is Leap Castle near Roscrea. Another is Loftus Hall in Wexford – a ghostly place where things go bump in the night. In these houses, lights flicker, strange noises can be heard and the atmosphere is eerie and chilly.

It certainly takes an adventurous soul to visit a spooky place like this. Are you brave enough?

The Yawl is a two-masted wooden sailing boat. Originally it was used for fishing and transporting seaweed.

Razorbill

The Galway Hooker was built to suit the rugged bays of the West Coast.

Cormorant

Capsize!

Optimist Racing Dinghies

Currachs have been used by fishermen for over 2,000 years.

Go Boating

Around our beautiful little island, you can find so many locations to go out on a boat. There are hundreds of inland lakes to launch and sail on too. Sailing boats come in all sizes, from small dinghies that you can sail by yourself, up to large yachts and catamarans with several crew members.

Traditional Irish boats include the Galway Hooker, with its eye-catching red sails, the Yawl and the Currach. You can see them in action at boat races, regattas and festivals. You can learn to sail for fun, gently bobbing along on a warm summer evening, or go racing across a bay in a near gale.

Sailors wear the right clothes for their adventures. Keeping warm, but not necessarily dry, is important. Part of the fun of sailing a small boat is lots of splashes, if not a full-on dunk in the water, so a wetsuit helps to keep you warm. Another vital piece of equipment is the buoyancy aid which will keep you floating if you fall in. When you're ready, hoist the sail! We're heading out.

FARRELL

5 KEHOE

Dancing a three-handed reel

Flute

Fiddle

Bodhrán drum and stick

14

Dancing At the Fleadh Cheoil

'Fleadh Cheoil' is an Irish phrase that means 'music festival'. At the fleadh you will hear the very best Irish traditional musicians and see dancers on the street. The location of the fleadh changes from year to year and thousands of people visit the town it is held in. Can you find out where it will be this year?

The festival is a huge celebration of Irish culture and celebration of Irish music and dance. If you feel adventurous you might like to join in some Irish dancing with your family at a céilí on the street. Maybe you can bring your own instrument and play along? Or you might just like to tap your toes to some incredible traditional music with the fiddle, accordion and the beat of the bodhrán.

Guitar

Mandolin

Harp

Concertina

Tin Whistle

Windsurfer

Riding the face of the wave.

Carving, or turning the board on a wave.

Riding through the barrel of the wave.

A surfer who rides with their right foot forward is known as a goofy foot.

16

Surf an Atlantic Wave

Thanks to the wild Atlantic Ocean, the west coast of Ireland is home to some of the best surfing waves in the whole world. It may not be as warm as Hawaii, but that's where a warm wetsuit comes in handy.

Standing on a wave with the sea spray in your face and a board beneath your feet must be one of the best feelings in the world. You can learn to surf on safe beaches with small waves.

As you get more experience you can try out bigger waves. The very best surfers in Ireland surf on some of the biggest waves on the planet, like the world-famous Aileen's wave near the Cliffs of Moher.

And, of course, if you don't want to get wet yourself, it can be just as exciting to watch the surfers gliding down the face of a giant breaker, while you stay warm on the beach. Either way, get ready to be mesmerised at the sounds, sights and smells of the awesome Atlantic Ocean.

A blue flag means the beach is clean and safe.

Surfers wear wetsuits to keep warm.

Bottlenose dolphins enjoy surfing too.

Body boarding

The first manned hot air balloon was flown by the Montgolfier brothers in 1783.

Hot air balloons come in many shapes and sizes.

Trim Castle is a Norman Castle. Parts of it are over 800 years old.

The balloon or bag is also known as an envelope.

A Norman Knight!

The basket is called a gondola.

The ground crew stabilise the balloon until take off.

Ride in Hot Air Balloon

What could be better than a beautiful blue Irish sky? How about a beautiful sky filled with beautiful hot air balloons? Imagine soaring into the sky with just a wicker basket beneath your feet and balloon above your head. Take off at dawn and watch the countryside wake up. From curious cows in a field to tiny cars on roads stretching off into the distance, the world looks different from the perspective of a bird.

The very first passenger trip in a hot air balloon took place in 1783 in France, but today you can find hot air balloons taking off all over Ireland. There is even an Irish Hot Air Balloon Championship where you can see balloons of every shape, size and colour from around the world. Balloons regularly take off from Trim, Co. Meath.

Because they have no engines, the balloons fly along in the same direction as the wind. A balloon pilot can chart a course by changing the height of the balloon to take advantage of different wind speeds and directions. The pilot will choose exactly where to land before they even take off.

Are you ready to float up, up and away?

The pilot fills the balloon with hot air from the burner.

Seal Spotting

All around the coast of Ireland, you will find colonies of seals. These playful acrobats can often be spotted in harbours and around rocky beaches and headlands. Seals love to bask, lying on the rocks, before sliding into the water to catch fish, squid and shellfish for their dinner.

The most common seals are the Grey Seal and the Harbour Seal and they are a lot of fun to watch.

Seals are curious creatures and will follow boats to see what's going on.

Seals can hold their breath underwater for up to 30 minutes.

A male seal is called a bull.

A baby seal is called a pup.

A female seal is called a cow.

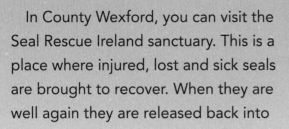

In County Wexford, you can visit the Seal Rescue Ireland sanctuary. This is a place where injured, lost and sick seals are brought to recover. When they are well again they are released back into the wild. If you see a sick or injured seal, you should never approach it. Instead, phone the seal sanctuary and the trained professionals will come to look after it.

On land, a group of seals is called a colony. At sea it is called a raft.

Seals are wild animals so keep well back when you are watching them.

Only trained seal rescuers should approach a seal.

This seal has recovered from an injury and is now returning to the wild.

Sometimes baby seals get lost or are abandoned. The rescue team look after them at the sanctuary until they are old enough to look after themselves.

Horse Trekking

The horse is one of the most popular animals in Ireland. Riding or trekking a trail on the back of a two-metre friend is a great way to see some Irish wilderness and enjoy an adventure.

If you're new to horse riding, an instructor will show you how to use the reins to help your horse go in the direction you want. They'll make sure all of your equipment is safe and sturdy. They'll also show you how to make your horse stop when you want it to!

Because you're sitting up so high, you'll get an amazing view when you hit the trail. You can find horse trekking in every county in Ireland with beautiful, well-trained horses to take you on your way. Giddy up!

Fox

Salmon

Kingfisher

Freshwater Mussels

Foxgloves are also known as Fairy Bells, Fairy Fingers & Fairy Thimbles.
But don't eat them!
They're poisonous.

22

Connemara Pony

Riding Hat

Riding Boots

Otter

Dipper

23

Island of Innisfree

A life jacket helps to keep you afloat if you fall in.

W.B. Yeats

Stand Up Paddle Boarding

'I will arise and go now, and go to Innisfree'. Those are the words of the great Irish poet, W.B. Yeats. When he wrote about going to Innisfree he probably didn't imagine that one day adventurers would travel out to the island on a Stand Up Paddle Board. The island is on Lough Gill in Sligo.

Stand Up Paddle Boarding is what you get when you combine surfing with kayaking. Although SUP boarding is a new and popular way to get out on the water, its roots go back thousands of years to Hawaiian and African culture.

Maybe Yeats would have appreciated this quiet and gentle way to travel to the island. Let's paddle!

Oh no! He's lost his balance.

Beginners start by paddling while kneeling on the board.

Swans

25

Alder Tree

Rothschild Giraffe

Grant's Zebra

Kafue Lechwe

Bison

A baby bison is called a calf.

Colombian Spider Monkey

Cheetah

Agile Gibbon

Meerkat

Indian Rhino

Chilean Flamingo

Sumatran Tiger

Ring-Tailed Lemur

Asiatic Lions

Go On Safari

Ireland is probably not the first place you think of when you hear the word 'safari'. However, there is a small island north of Cobh in Co. Cork and it is home to over 70 species of birds and animals from around the world. Lions, zebra, giraffe and monkeys all call this little island their home. It's called Fota Wildlife Park.

Fota is not about caged animals. Instead, where it's possible, you can see wild beasts roaming free, mixing with other animals. Watch the cheetahs in their special run as they hit their top speeds of 65 km per hour, see if you can hop as high as the kangaroos, or sit as still and alert as a cute little meerkat.

Dive a Shipwreck

If you love the ocean and the hidden mysteries that await below the waves, how about a scuba dive to a wrecked ship?

From a World War 2 German U-boat to a luxury ocean liner and a real life pirate ship, over the last few hundred years, many a vessel has met its unfortunate end beneath the waves around our coast.

Some wrecks are too dangerous while others are too far down to dive to, but amazing dive sites are found all around the coast which can be accessed by scuba divers looking for adventure.

Take a deep breath and let's descend into the depths!

Eel

Small octopus like to hide in dark secluded places.

A starfish can grow a replacement arm if it loses one.

Lophelia Coral

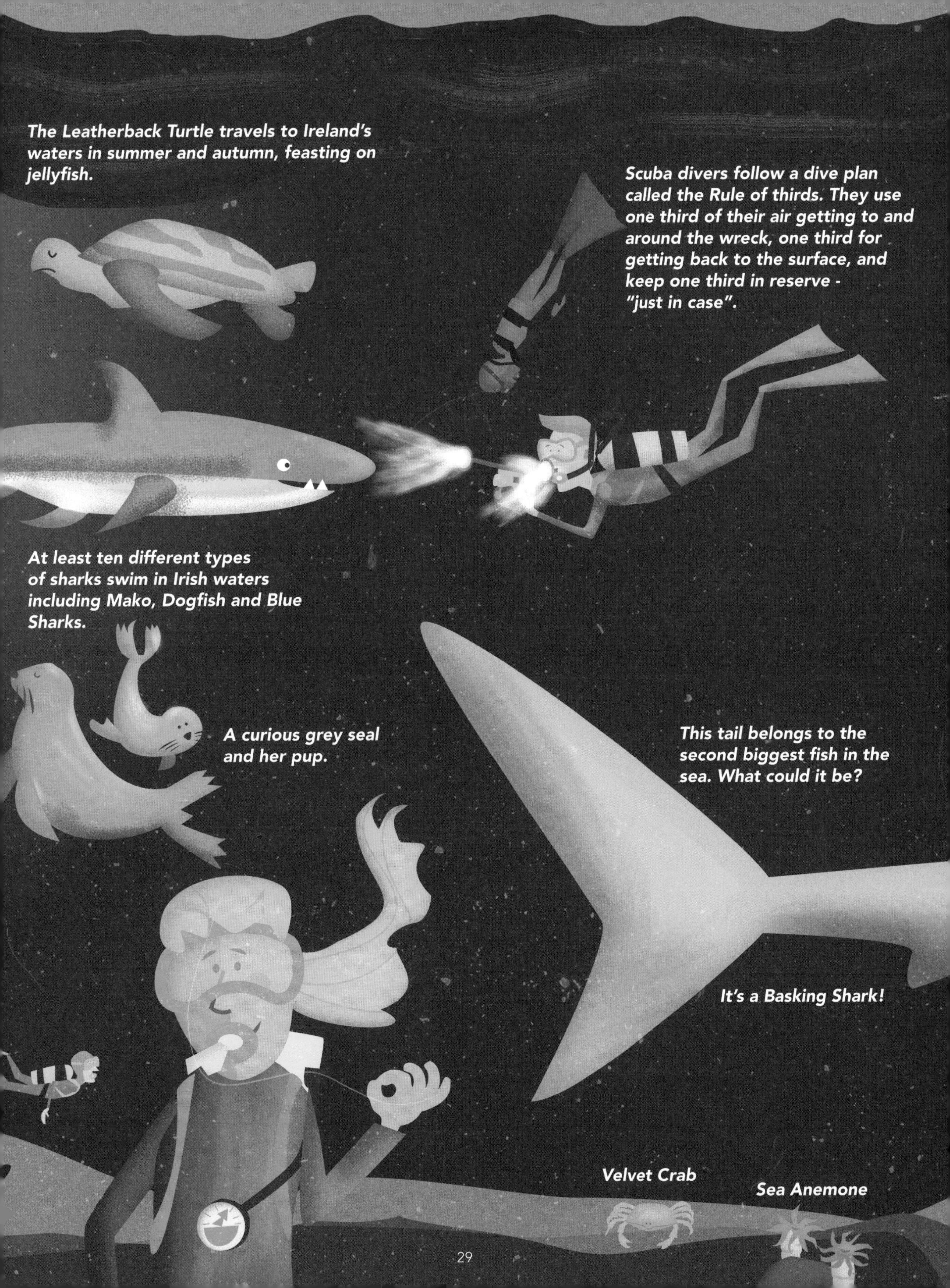

The Leatherback Turtle travels to Ireland's waters in summer and autumn, feasting on jellyfish.

Scuba divers follow a dive plan called the Rule of thirds. They use one third of their air getting to and around the wreck, one third for getting back to the surface, and keep one third in reserve - "just in case".

At least ten different types of sharks swim in Irish waters including Mako, Dogfish and Blue Sharks.

A curious grey seal and her pup.

This tail belongs to the second biggest fish in the sea. What could it be?

It's a Basking Shark!

Velvet Crab

Sea Anemone

St Patrick's Day

St Patrick is the patron saint of Ireland and he is famous for banishing the snakes from the country and for using a shamrock to explain Christianity. Almost every town and village in Ireland celebrates St Patrick's Day on the 17th of March with a parade. Some village parades are tiny with a few tractors and the local school band putting on a show.

Other parades taking place in Dublin, Cork and Limerick are huge, with bands coming from all over the world to play along on the day we celebrate our Irishness.

You can go along for the adventure and wear a fake leprechaun beard, have shamrocks painted on your face and see if you can see St Patrick himself mingling with the crowd.

For safety, climbers wear
helmets and harnesses.

Sea stacks are pillars of rock. They
are formed when crashing waves and
wind cause a piece of land to crack,
weaken and break away.

The climbers get to the
sea stack by dinghy.

Special rock-climbing shoes give
the climbers extra grip on the
slippy cliff-face.

Hill Walking and Sea Stack Climbing

How would you feel about dangling from a cliff with crashing waves below?
Does that make your toes curl or fill you with excitement? For some daredevil
adventurers, climbing a sea stack is a challenging and rewarding way to spend
their time.

   The Donegal coast is home to many stunning sea stacks jutting out of the
Atlantic. For professional, fully trained climbers, these giant outcrops of rock
are the ultimate challenge. First, they have to get to the base of the stack by
boat and then the slow ascent to the top begins. Using climbing ropes and
equipment, the climber makes their way bit by bit toward the top.

Great Skua

Pod of Killer Whales

Once they've made it to the top, there is just enough time to look around and enjoy the view before the next adventure begins. Getting back down again! The climber creates an anchor at the top, leans out over the edge and abseils down the face of the stack.

If you'd prefer to keep your feet on solid ground while still getting an amazing view from the top, hill-walking is a brilliant adventure that can be enjoyed by everyone.

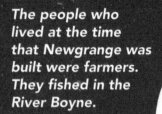

The people who lived at the time that Newgrange was built were farmers. They fished in the River Boyne.

Visit an Ancient Tomb

Imagine visiting a tomb older than the pyramids! Around Brú na Bóinne in Co. Meath, there are several ancient tombs that you can visit. The most famous is Newgrange. This Stone Age tomb is older than the pyramids and was built by early settlers to Ireland.

Light comes through the roof-box above the entrance way.

Carved artwork

34

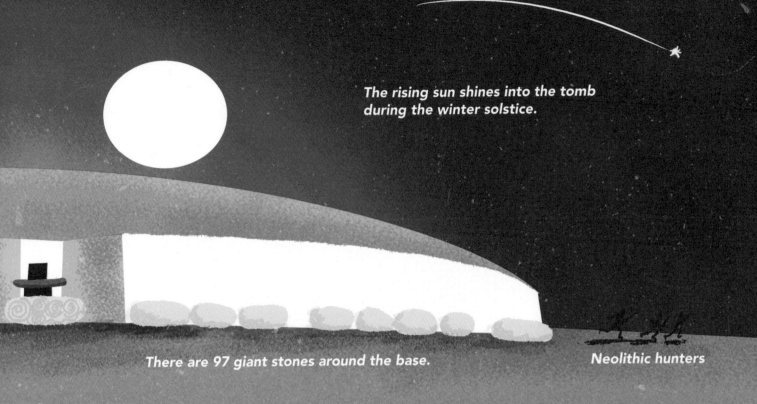

The rising sun shines into the tomb during the winter solstice.

There are 97 giant stones around the base.

Neolithic hunters

Newgrange is a very special place. It's known as a passage tomb. The people who lived at that time designed it so that once a year, at the winter solstice – the 21st December, the light from the rising sun would come in through a small hole above the doorway and light up the whole tomb.

Today when you go to the Brú na Bóinne visitor centre, you can go right inside the tomb and see artwork carved into the walls that is thousands of years old.

The entrance stone is beautifully carved.

Once inside the guide will switch off all the lights (and it's pitch dark) and demonstrate how the sunlight slowly filters in and reaches the burial chamber where you're standing. It's mystical and magical.

Kayak Beneath the Stars

Kayaking is fun at any time of the day, but for a very special adventure, how about trying a moonlit paddle?

Lough Hyne in West Cork is the only inland saltwater lake in Europe. It is connected to the Atlantic Ocean by a slim channel of water. As the light of the day fades, you can push your kayak out into the lake and paddle silently into the night. As the sun goes down, thousands of stars begin to twinkle above your head.

At certain times of the year something unique and special happens. The tiny marine life starts to let out light underwater. This is known as bio-luminescence. As your paddle moves through the water, thousands of tiny bubbles light up. With the moonlight and stars reflecting on the surface of the water, and the tiny sparkling beneath, it seems like Mother Nature is putting on a light show, just for you.

Bio-luminescence

Orion's Belt

**MacGillycuddy's Reeks,
Ireland's highest mountain range.**

All the Fun of the Fair

Every summer in Ireland, towns and villages are home to outdoor fairs, family festivals and parties. From air shows to haymaking, flower and river festivals, there is a ton of fun and adventure to be enjoyed.

The oldest, and one of the most famous fairs, is the Puck Fair. Every August, in the mountains near Killorglin Co. Kerry, a wild male goat is taken from the mountain and brought to the town. A young girl who is known as the Queen of the Puck, crowns him King of the Goats or King Puck. When the fair is over he is brought back to his mountain home.

The Puck King of
the Goats.

The Queen of
the Puck.

A vet makes sure that the goat
is well cared for and looked
after while the fair is on.

Seabirds & Sea Life on Skellig

Imagine an inhospitable rocky island jutting out of the wild Atlantic sea. The only things on the island are the seagulls and puffin nests, and the ancient stone huts of monks who lived here over 1,000 years ago.

The place you're imagining is called Skellig Michael and it lies just off the South West coast of Ireland.

Monks lived in stone Beehive Huts.

Ancient Monk. Or could it be a Jedi?

Fulmar

Rabbit

Arctic Tern

There are over 600 steps on the steep climb to the top.

This is a remote but magical place. Often the seas are stormy and wild and you can only get onto the island when it is calm. When you arrive, there is a long winding set of steps. The steps are steep and there is no handrail. But, if you are adventurous enough to brave the seas, the wind and the steps, you will be rewarded with a most wondrous view.

Nearby is Little Skellig island and off in the distance you'll see the mainland of Ireland. Are you brave enough to venture out to Skellig Michael?

The Gannet is Ireland's largest seabird.

Little Skellig

Skellig Michael towers 218 metres above sea level.

You can get to the island by boat when the weather is calm.

Puffin

Sculpt a Super Sand Castle

On every beach in Ireland there's an opportunity to build your own super sand castle. Or maybe you would like to sculpt a dinosaur or a character from your favourite fairy tale out of sand?

If you fancy a bit of a competition, you could try your skills at one of the many sand sculpting and sand castle competitions that take place around the country.

Once such event is the Sand Castle Championship at Bettystown Co. Meath. Here some of the best sand castle makers and sand sculptors get together to compete to see who

Ringed Plover

Who let the dog loose on the beach?

The Sphinx

Sandcastle Building tools of the trade

Straws

Melon Baller

Spatula

Paintbrush

Spade

Funnel

Bucket

can make the most amazing creation out of sand. From two-storey sand mansions to giant works of art, if it can be built with sand and water you'll find it here. And guess what? If you go along there's nothing to stop you from making your own masterpiece on the beach too! You might even get some tips from the pros.

Get your bucket, spade and imagination ready and start building your wonderful sand sculptures.

Common Tern

Don't forget your sunscreen.

Aurora Borealis is the scientific name for the 'Northern Lights'.

The aurora often look like 'curtains' of light, which are constantly changing shape.

Catch A Glimpse Of the Northern Lights

The Northern Lights are an amazing sight in the night sky. Usually they are only seen in countries near the Arctic Circle, but sometimes they can be seen farther south. In Ireland, the best chance to catch a glimpse of the Northern Lights is in the northern counties of Donegal,

'Aurora' comes from the Roman goddess of dawn and the Latin word for 'sunrise'.

Mussenden Temple

of Donegal, Derry and Antrim. To see them, you would need to stay up late at night, wrap up warm and go outdoors away from city and town lights.

There is, of course, no guarantee that you will see this amazing sight, but if you're very, very lucky, and the weather is just right, you might just get to see Mother Nature's most spectacular light show.

Rock Island

Brannock Islands

Horse and cart is a good way to see the islands and hear stories from the driver.

Seal Colony

Kilronan

Inis Mór (Inishmore)

Atlantic Ocean

Dún Aonghasa is an ancient stone fort on the edge of dramatic 100 metre high cliffs.

Cliff diving at the Wormhole, or the Serpent's Lair.

Island Hopping

From Tory Island in the north, to Cape Clear Island in the south, there are many inhabited and uninhabited islands around Ireland that you can visit in search of adventure.

The Aran Islands lie off the west coast of Ireland. The three main islands are Inis Mór, the big island, Inis Meáin, the middle island, and Inis Oirr, the east or rear island. The islands are home to ancient forts, some of the highest cliffs in Ireland and even a shipwreck.

Most people who live on the islands speak Irish and some still live a traditional way of life that you will no longer see on the mainland of Ireland.

You can swim, cycle, kayak, hike, run, watch seals play, step back in time. And when you're feeling tired you can look out at the amazing views across the Atlantic Ocean.

Swimming in the crystal clear water.

You can visit the islands by light plane or boat.

To Galway

Fort of Conchúir
Fort of Fergal

Curragh

**Inis Meáin
(Inishmaan)**

**Inis Oirr
(Inisheer)**

To Doolin
Co. Clare

The Plessey Freighter was washed ashore on a stormy night in 1960.

N
W   E
S

Dedication

**For my Mam and Dad, Vera and Joe,
for giving me a world of adventures.**

Jennifer Farley is an illustrator, designer and author from Dublin.
Her work has been published in books, magazines and even on the side of
a lorry. She lives in Westmeath with her husband and dogs. Her favourite
colour is deep red. www.JenFarley.com

First published 2018 by The O'Brien Press Ltd,
12 Terenure Road East, Rathgar, D06 HD27, Dublin 6, Ireland.
Tel: +353 1 4923333; Fax: +353 1 4922777
E-mail: books@obrien.ie
Website: www.obrien.ie
The O'Brien Press is a member of Publishing Ireland.

ISBN: 978-1-84717-971-5

Copyright for text © Jennifer Farley 2018
Copyright for typesetting, layout, design © The O'Brien Press Ltd 2018

10 9 8 7 6 5 4 3 2 1

22 21 20 19 18

Layout and design: The O'Brien Press Ltd.

Printed by EDELVIVES, Spain.
The paper in this book is produced using pulp from managed forests.

Published in

DUBLIN
UNESCO
City of Literature